TADPOLES

BETSY JAMES

Dutton Children's Books · New York

Published in the United States by Dutton Children's Books,

a division of Penguin Putnam Books for Young Readers

345 Hudson Street, New York, New York 10014

http://www.penguinputnam.com/yreaders/index.htm

Designed by Alan Carr

Printed in Hong Kong

First Edition

ISBN 0-525-46197-3

1 3 5 7 9 10 8 6 4 2

For Mimi the Frog Lady, of course

Last fall I got a little brother. All he could do was yell and smell and drool. Ma carried him everywhere. I had to walk.

One afternoon in spring, we walked to the pond.

"Carry me!" I said.

But Ma said, "Sweetie, I have to carry Davey."

And when we sat down, Davey got to sit in her lap.

If we held very still, frogs began to sing. I waded to a rock and looked in the water. Something shiny floated in the weeds.

"Look!" I called. "Little balls of jelly!"

"Those are eggs," said Ma. "A mother frog laid them."

"They've got dots inside," I said.

"Those dots will grow legs and turn into frogs," said Ma. "All animals look like dots when they're just beginning to grow. People do, too."

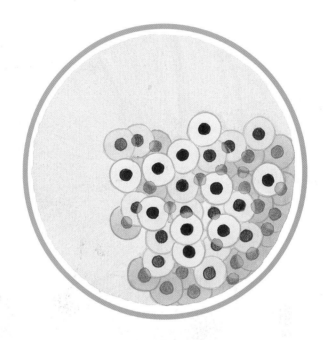

"Was I a dot?" I asked.

"Yes, when you were inside me. Then you grew legs and arms and turned into a baby, and got born."

"Was Davey a dot?" I asked.

"He was."

"The legs he grew don't work," I said.

"Wait and see," said Ma. "He'll learn to walk."

But I said, "I'd rather have a frog than a brother."

Ma smiled. "Scoop up a few eggs, then," she said. "We'll take them home in a plastic bag and watch how they grow. But, Molly, when they've turned into frogs, we'll have to bring them back to their pond. Okay?"

"Okay," I promised.

When we walked back home, Ma carried Davey, and I carried some eggs floating in pond water.

I put them in my old fishbowl and watched them. But they didn't turn into frogs. They didn't do anything.

After a week I lifted Davey up to see. "That's what you used to be," I told him. "A dot."

I looked again. "Hey!" I shouted. "My dots are growing tails!"

Ma came to look. "A frog's egg has to turn into a tadpole first," she said. "That's a baby frog. The way Davey has to be a baby first, and then a boy."

Inside the jelly, my tadpoles wiggled. Soon they wiggled themselves right out into the water.

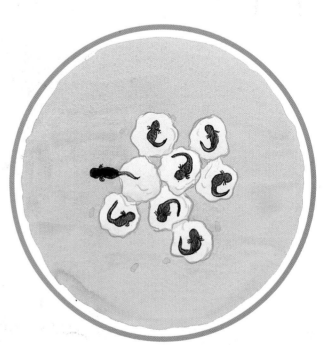

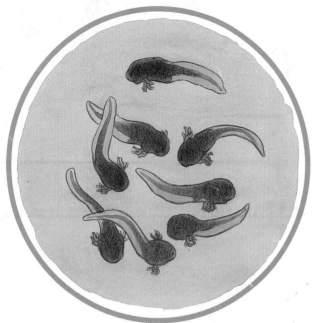

The jelly fell apart, and the tadpoles swam around. Ma said, "Their frilly gills are to breathe with under the water, like fish."

Every day I lifted Davey up to see. I had to catch him first, because he was learning to crawl.

"It's nice of you to show Davey your tadpoles," said Ma.

I said, "I'm teaching him to be a boy instead of a baby."

I brought my tadpoles fresh water and plants from the pond. They nibbled the green fuzzy algae that grew on the plants.

They got bigger. Their gills disappeared, and they came up to breathe the air. Two stumpy lumps grew next to their tails.

"That's where their legs will be," said Dad.

On the Fourth of July we went camping all weekend. When we got home my tadpoles had grown tiny back legs.

"They kick like Davey," said Dad.

All summer my tadpoles swam and swam. Davey crawled and crawled. My tadpoles ate lettuce, and even meat if I hung it in their water on a string. Davey ate Fig Newtons, and rubbed them in my hair.

"Tad!" he said, and tried to crawl up on my table.

I caught him. "*My* tadpoles," I said. "Pretty soon they'll grow front legs. They'll learn to jump."

"When they can jump, they'll be frogs," said Ma. "Then we'll take them back to their pond."

"Not yet," I said. "They're still babies."

But next morning, when I lifted Davey up, I saw my tadpoles were growing front legs.

Summer was almost over. Davey could stand up. He could walk, but only if he held on to my fingers. He wanted to practice walking all the time.

My tadpoles' tails disappeared. I put a rock in their bowl, and as their legs got stronger they learned to crawl up onto it.

"They look like frogs now," I told Davey one morning. "But they still can't jump."

"Ump!" said Davey. He pointed.

One little frog jumped right out of the fishbowl.

Gently, Ma caught it. She covered the bowl with a cloth.

"All grown up," she said.

"No!" I said.

"They're ready to be big frogs," said Ma.

"I don't care!"

"I know you don't want to take them back, Molly," said Ma.

"Let's enjoy them today. Tomorrow we can walk to the pond."

"Walk!" said Davey, and pulled on my fingers.

"Grow up," I said. "Walk by yourself." I pulled my fingers
away. He sat down on his bottom and cried.

That night Ma sat with me and patted my back.

"You love your froggies a lot," she said. "But would a big frog be happy in a tiny fishbowl?"

"We could get a great big fishbowl," I said.

"It wouldn't have trees and birds and dragonflies, like their real home," said Ma. "They need room to jump and lay more eggs, so there will be frogs next summer."

"But they're *mine*," I said.

"Are they?" said Ma. "Or do they belong to themselves?"

Next morning we took the path to the pond. Ma carried Davey. I carried my frogs, so carefully, in a plastic bowl with a towel over it so they couldn't jump out.

Ma put Davey down and held his hand.

I stood on the rock with my bowl of frogs and cried.

"Molly," said Ma. "It's time to let them go."

I said, "*I don't want to!*"

Davey let go of Ma's hand. "MOLLY, WALK!" he said.

He held out his arms to me. All by himself, he wobbled down the shore, splashed through the water, and crashed into my legs.

The bowl flew into the air. All together, Davey and the frogs and I went SPLOOSH!

Ma splashed into the pond and grabbed us both.

Davey howled. I yelled, "He made me drop my frogs!"

"I know," said Ma. She held me tight. "But look how well you taught him! He walked all by himself, straight to you."

Davey stopped howling. The pond was quiet.

"My frogs aren't singing," I said.

"Not till spring," said Ma.

"Will I hear them then?"

"For sure."

We started home. "Carry me!" I said. "Davey can walk now."

"Could you take turns?" said Ma.

And that's what we did.

ABOUT FROGS

STAGES

EGG

12 DAYS

4 WEEKS

9 WEEKS

12 WEEKS

14 WEEKS

16 WEEKS

The frog in this book is the most common North American frog, the northern leopard frog. Like all frogs (and toads), its babies are called *tadpoles*.

A frog begins its life swimming in the water and breathing with gills like a fish; then it changes into a land-living animal that breathes the air with lungs, the way we do. The time to collect frog eggs is in the spring or summer, when frogs make the *brrr*-ing, trilling noise we call "singing." Look for their eggs in wet places: streams, ponds, even irrigation ditches. First, though, please find out whether collecting frog eggs is legal where you live. In some areas, frogs have become scarce, and people are not allowed to collect even a few eggs.

If collecting is allowed, here are some rules:

• Take only a few eggs, and only from a place that has many eggs. Wash your hands first. Take plenty of extra pond water home with the eggs.

• Please don't touch your tadpoles or frogs (except in an emergency, as Molly's mother did). Frogs breathe partly through their skins, and chemicals or dirt on your hands can harm them.

• Put the eggs and water in a large bowl, and keep it in the shade. Change the pond water every few days; tip out most of the old water (but not the tadpoles) and pour in the new water. Never use water from the faucet.

• Watch your tadpoles carefully. They may grow faster or slower than the ones in this book, because the temperature of the place where you live will determine how fast they develop. They may be a different color—or even grow into a different kind of frog, since most frog eggs look a lot alike.

• At first your tadpoles will nibble on everything, especially the fuzzy algae that grows on water plants. When they are a little bigger they will eat tiny bits of lettuce. You can feed them a little raw meat the way Molly did—but don't leave it in the water long, because it will spoil quickly.

• As their legs grow and their tails shorten, they will stop eating. When their tails are almost gone they will start to eat again—but they will eat only live, wiggling animals like flies, worms, and beetles. You must take them back to their home pond so they can find the right food. Always take the grown-up frogs back to the same pond where you got the eggs.

• Some of your tadpoles may die before they finish growing. Of all the eggs laid by a mother frog, only a few reach adulthood. Some simply die, and others are eaten by birds, fish, and beetles, to help these animals grow.

• Tadpoles and frogs eat mosquitoes and many other insect pests. They are beautiful and fun to watch, and make us happy with their singing. Please help them by taking care of the ponds and streams that are their homes.